FIRST GRADE

More Adventures of the Superkids

BY
PLEASANT T. ROWLAND

STORIES WRITTEN BY
VALERIE TRIPP

ILLUSTRATED BY
MERYL HENDERSON

DEVELOPED BY
ROWLAND READING FOUNDATION

ZB Zaner-Bloser

A Highlights Company

ISBN 978-1-61436-578-5

888.378.9258
zaner-bloser.com

Printed in the United States of America

7 8 9 10 11 12 13 14 15   25170   26 25 24 23 22 21

Contents

Unit 9

Memory Words boy two about girl over before four

5

"Your play is good, Icky," said Doc. "But wouldn't a talent show be better? Then we could do the acts we want to do."

"O.K.!" said Icky. "My play wasn't a hit. But a talent show will be."

Save The Trees!
Help the
Big Tree Fund.

The Spingle Spangle Talent Show

Chapter 1

The Superkids were putting on a show.
Doc made a list of jobs and acts.

The Spingle Spangle Talent Show

1. **Doc** Set up benches for the show.

2. **Hot Rod** Fix up the bus for the show.

3. **Lily** Sell tickets.

4. **Cass** Get stuff for the show.

5. **Sal** Sing a song.

6. **Tic, Tac, Toc** Tell jokes.

7. **Oswald, Alf, Icky,** and **Frits** Do a band act.

The boys and girls had lots to do
before the show. But Ettabetta
sat on the bus.

"My name isn't on the list," said
Ettabetta. "Doc didn't want me in
the show."

Chapter 2

The show began.

"We have four fantastic acts," said Doc. "Let's begin with Sal."

Sal got up on stilts. He sang a song about animals. He hopped and jumped, but he didn't tip over.

"That was terrific!" said Doc.

"No it wasn't! It was rotten," said Ettabetta.

"But the show is not over," said Doc. "Next we have three girls who will tell us about chickens."

"Those jokes weren't any good!"
said Ettabetta.

Doc said, "We have two acts to go.
Next up is the Octopus Band!"

Oswald sang. The boys in the band
banged, beeped, and buzzed along.

"Thanks, Octopus Band," said Doc.

Ettabetta couldn't stand it. The show
was ending, and she hadn't gotten
to be in it!

Chapter 3

Doc said, "We saved the best act for last. It's Ettabetta!"

Ettabetta didn't come.

"Where is Ettabetta?" asked Doc.

"We haven't seen her," said Tic.

"I am on the bus," said Ettabetta.

"Aren't you planning to do your act?" asked Doc.

"No!" said Ettabetta. "My name wasn't on the list!"

"It wasn't?" Doc said. "I didn't mean to forget you. Couldn't you still do your act? The show will flop without it."

"Well, O.K.," said Ettabetta.

Amazing Ettabetta

"I am an acrobat!" said Ettabetta. And she did a handstand.

She did leg splits.

She did backbends.

She did handsprings and flips.

"What a fantastic ending for the Spingle Spangle Talent Show!" said Doc.

Buster Is Back!

 Bringgg!

 "Hi!"

 "Hi, Cass. This is Frits. I have something to tell you. You remember Buster the pigeon, don't you?"

 "Yes, I remember Buster from last summer. He broke his wing. You helped him get better."

 "Well, Buster is back. He is making a nest in my attic."

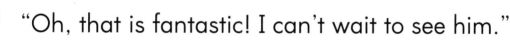 "Oh, that is fantastic! I can't wait to see him."

"Why don't you come over? You can take a look at him."

 "O.K. Let's tell the other kids. We can meet in your attic."

 "Good plan! The others won't want to miss seeing Buster."

 "See you in a bit."

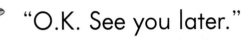 "O.K. See you later."

Buster's Surprise

Chapter 1

The Superkids went to Frits's attic to see Buster the pigeon.

"Look at Buster!" said Frits. "Isn't he fantastic?"

"Yes," said Cass. "But I don't think Buster is a boy."

"What?" said Frits.

"Buster is a girl. Look in the nest," said Cass, smiling.

"An egg!" said Frits.

"How long before the egg hatches?" asked Hot Rod.

"I have a book about pigeons," said Oswald. "It can tell us when the egg will hatch."

Cass, Oswald, and Frits left to get the book. The rest of the kids went home.

Here is what it said in Oswald's book:

1. A pigeon makes a nest
   out of sticks and twigs.

2. A pigeon has two eggs.

3. It takes 17 days before
   the eggs hatch.

"But there weren't two eggs in Buster's nest.
There was only one," said Cass.

The kids went back to check Buster's nest.

"Look," said Oswald. "There are TWO eggs!"

"Don't tell the other kids," said Frits. "Let's bring them back over here just before the eggs hatch."

"O.K. We won't tell," said Cass and Oswald.

Chapter 2

For 17 days, Buster sat on the eggs. On the last day, the Superkids came to visit Buster. The Superkids waited and waited.

"I can't wait any longer," said Icky. "Why won't the eggs hatch?"

Just then, Buster fluttered her wings and stepped off the nest.

"Oh, look!" said Hot Rod. "There are two eggs!"

"Buster has twins," giggled Lily.

Then it happened. *Peck. Peck.* Two little bills pecked at the eggshells.

"You can do it, little pigeons," said Cass.

The little pigeons kicked and thrashed. The eggshells began to crack and split. At last, the little pigeons fell out.

The kids clapped and smiled.

"The little pigeons are fantastic!" said Frits.
"What can we name them?"

"What about Hot and Rod?" joked Hot Rod.

"Let's not, you wing-ding," said Cass
with a grin.

"That is it!" said Lily. "Why don't we
name them Wing and Ding?"

"Yes, I like that," said Frits. "Hi, Wing!
Hi, Ding!"

Unit 10

Memory Words   down   too   work   many   first

My Happy Rainy Day

In the summer when it's rainy,
Do not sit inside.
Stomp in messy, splashy puddles.
Run and jump and slide!

Grab big globs of mucky mud
And make a lumpy pie.
Quack back to funny ducks
That fly by in the sky.

Tilt your chin up. Lift your hands up.
Feel rain on your skin.
Spin until you are quite dizzy.
Grin a silly grin.

If the other children ask you,
"Why won't you get dry?"
Yell, "Getting wet is fun!
I like rain. That's why!"

In Case of Rain

Rainy Day Projects

From Superkids' Brains

A Monster Mask
by Tic and Cass

You will need:
- a paper bag
- scissors
- paint
- tape
- paper

1. Cut holes in the paper bag.
2. Paint the mask.
3. Tape paper teeth and funny ears on the mask.
4. Cut flaps on the sides of the bag.

Put on the mask and act like a monster!

flap

flap

Leapfrog
by Sal, Tac, and Alf

You will need:
• plenty of kids

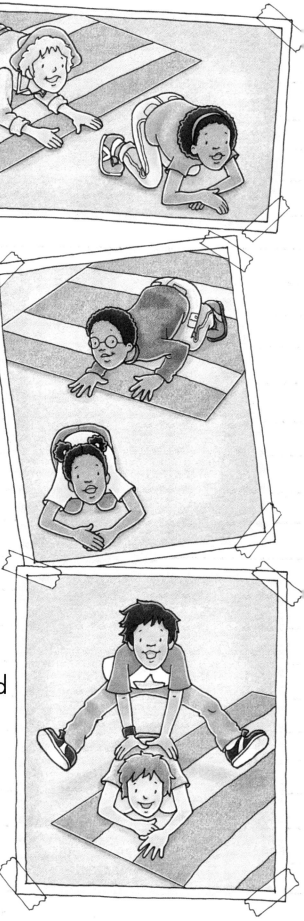

1. Tell the kids to scrunch down in a line.
2. Go to the back of the line.
3. Jump like a frog over each person.
4. When you get to the front of the line, stay there and scrunch down, too.
5. Tell the last person in line to jump over each kid and then scrunch down at the front of the line.
6. Play until each kid has hopped over the rest of the kids.

Odd Socks
by Ettabetta, Oswald, and Cass

You will need:
- socks for each kid
- things with odd shapes
  that will fit in the socks

1. Put one thing in each sock.
2. Hand each kid a sock.
3. Ask your pals to feel the
   socks and try to name what
   is in them.

Leaf Prints
by Frits, Tic, and Lily

You will need:
- a big leaf
- a flat stick
- a toothbrush
- paint
- paper

1. Lay the leaf on the paper.
2. Dip the brush in the paint.
3. Rub the stick across the brush. This may be messy, but it is really fun.

4. Peel the leaf off the paper.
5. Let the paint dry.

Leaf prints make nifty gifts!

Feed Beanbags to a Dragon
by Icky and Doc

You will need:
- a big box
- paint
- five beanbags
- scissors

1. Cut a hole in a big box.
2. Paint a hungry dragon on it.
3. Get five beanbags.
4. Pick two teams. Have three kids on each team.
5. Make a line three feet from the dragon.

How to Play:
The first kid on one team stands at the line and tosses five beanbags at the dragon.

Keep track of how many bags go in the hole.

Next, a kid from the other team tosses beanbags at the dragon. Keep going until every kid has had a try. The team that feeds the biggest number of beanbags to the dragon wins.

Cass Takes the Cake

"What are you making?" Toc asked.

"I am making a cake," said Cass.

"I liked the yummy cake you baked for Gert," Toc said.
"Is this one even yummier?"

"No, but I'm taking it with us to the lake," said Cass.

"What?" said Toc. "You are joking! We are hiking to the lake. You can't bring a cake. It will be a mess!"

Cass smiled. "I can bring this cake," she said. She held up a little cake shaped like a leaf. "This is a seed cake for the robins!"

Golly Helps

Chapter 1

The Superkids were camping at a lake.

"Let's set up camp first," said Lily.
"Then we will eat dinner."

Golly wanted to help, too.

Hot Rod was raking. Golly jumped into the neat piles Hot Rod had made.

Hot Rod groaned. "I just raked those!" he said. "Go away, Golly!"

Lily was setting up the tent. Golly ran over to help. His feet got stuck in the ropes.

"Golly!" said Lily. "You aren't helping. Go away!"

She seemed grumpier than Hot Rod, so Golly left quickly.

Golly tried to help Cass make dinner.

"Golly, you are the messiest dog!" yelled Cass. "Get lost!"

Cass seemed grumpier than Lily, so Golly left quickly.

Frits was fishing. Golly wanted to help.
But he tipped over the basket of fish.

"Golly, you are a pest!" said Frits.
"Get out of here!"

Chapter 2

Golly gave up and ran off. The
Superkids didn't want his help.
It was the grumpiest he had
ever seen them.

Then Golly spotted a little boy
waving his hands.

"Help! I dropped my truck!"
yelled the boy.

Golly jumped in the lake.
SPLASH! He got the truck and
swam back to the boy.

"Thanks, Dog!" said the boy. Then he patted Golly, and Golly wagged his tail.

The boy gave Golly the rest of his hot dog. Golly ate it fast. It was the yummiest snack!

Golly began to feel happier.

Then Golly spotted some kids in a tugging contest. He ran over and grabbed the rope with his teeth. He tugged and tugged. Golly liked helping the kids.

The other team began slipping
and sliding. After two big tugs,
those kids fell down.

"Yay! We win!" yelled Golly's team.
"Thanks, Dog!"

"Good work, Dog," said one girl. "It was a lot easier to win with your help."

The girl gave Golly some dinner. He ate it fast. It was the yummiest dinner!

After dinner, the kids gave Golly many pats. "You can help us any time!" the kids said.

Chapter 3

Golly went back to the Superkids.

"Golly, where were you?" asked Hot Rod. "We felt bad that we yelled at you."

"Yes," said Cass. "We saved some leftovers for you."

Golly just stuck up his nose.

Frits said, "Golly, you need to help us finish these leftovers."

But Golly was getting sleepier and sleepier. He had finished his helping for the day. It was time to rest.

Unit 11

Memory Words   their   now   always   because   been

It's So Hot!

 "It's so hot! I'm melting."

 "We're melting, too."

 "Look at Golly. He's panting."

 "I have good news. My mom said she'll drive us to the beach."

 "Yay! What a mom!"

 "She's fantastic!"

 "My dad said he'll pack a picnic for us."

 "Way to go, Doc's dad!"

 "Thanks for asking your mom to take us, Doc."

"You're welcome!"

"The beach has a big lake. We'll go swimming."

 "It'll feel good to get wet."

 "I'll be the first one to jump in the lake!"

 "No, you won't. You'll have to beat me to be first."

 "Let's go!"

61

The Wish

Chapter 1

"Ug!" said Oswald. "We always bring too much stuff to the beach. But it's a terrific spot for swimming."

"Last one in the lake is a rotten egg!" yelled Ettabetta.

The kids splashed in the lake until Doc's mom yelled, "Lunch!"

"Thanks," said Sal. "We're very hungry. I think I could eat a whale!"

"You're always hungry!" joked Tic.

The kids ate their lunches. Then Doc passed a box of fortune cookies.

"I liked the notes we got in the other fortune cookies," said Doc. "Let's see what are in these cookies."

Doc's fortune said,

Hug a girl with freckles. She'll bring you good luck.

"Hug Cass because she's got freckles," said Hot Rod.

Hot Rod's fortune said,

Run and sing and always be glad.

"It'll be fun to do that," said Hot Rod.

Oswald's fortune said,

This is your lucky day. You'll get your wish.

"Quick, make a wish,"
said Ettabetta.

"I can't think of one now,"
said Oswald. "I'll save it."

Chapter 2

After lunch, Oswald and Ettabetta looked at the boats.

"I have never been on a boat," said Oswald. "I wish I could go sailing."

"<u>That</u> is your wish!" said Ettabetta. "I hope you get it. We don't have a boat. But you could float on a tube."

So Oswald floated on the tube. He felt sleepier and sleepier. Then he fell asleep.

After a while, Doc's mom said, "We'll have to pack up now. It's time to go."

Suddenly Ettabetta yelled, "Look at Oswald! He's in the middle of the lake!"

The kids screamed and yelled.
But Oswald was still asleep.

A gull screamed. *Screech! Screech!*
It landed by the tube.

SPLASH!

Oswald woke up.

Chapter 3

"Oh, no!" Oswald groaned. "I'll never get back! My fortune said this was my lucky day. But look at the mess I'm in now!" He yelled, "Help! Help!"

"Look!" said Ettabetta. "There is a girl in a sailboat. She's close to Oswald. She'll pick him up, and he'll be safe."

The girl sailed up to Oswald.
She helped him get in the boat.

"Thanks," said Oswald.

"I'm glad I could help you,"
said the girl. "But now you'll
have to help me. Because it's so
windy, I need a hand sailing."

"I'm happy to help," said Oswald.

The girl gave Oswald a life vest. He held on to a rope. The wind filled the sails. The boat went flying across the lake. Oswald didn't want the trip to end.

When the boat landed on the beach,
Oswald hopped out. He thanked the girl.

"Oswald," said Ettabettta. "Your wish
came true!"

"Yes," said Oswald. "This really has been
my lucky day!"

You and Me and the Superkids

Hot Rod spotted this ad in the paper:

Happy Land is now open!

- Go on super fast rides!
- Pet cute baby animals!
- Tap your feet to terrific music!

Get happy at Happy Land!

Hot Rod showed the ad to his dad.

"Look at the fun things you can do at Happy Land," said Hot Rod.

"Do you mean fun things <u>you</u> can do or <u>I</u> can do?" asked Hot Rod's dad.

"Fun things you <u>and</u> I can do," said Hot Rod. "You like to go fast, too."

"That's true," his dad said. "O.K. You and I will drive over there next week."

"<u>And</u> the Superkids?" asked Hot Rod.

Hot Rod's dad smiled. "Yes," he said. "You, me, <u>and</u> the Superkids."

We made this scrapbook after a fun trip to Happy Land. We hope you have as much fun reading it as we had making it!

This shows us when we first got to Happy Land. Hot Rod's mom and dad drove us. We couldn't wait to go on the rides.

Frits and Doc went on a ride named Down the River. The boat zipped down a steep hill. *SPLASH!* Frits and Doc got very wet.

I'll bring my swim trunks next time!

Down the River
Admit One

I'm soaked, but it was fun!

Hit 5 bottles and win a big prize!

Sal got a tiger because he tipped over five bottles.

Lily, Toc, and Icky didn't hit very many bottles. But the man gave them paper hats.

You're a winner!

Grrr! I like my tiger!

At least we got fun hats.

80

Here we are in the Monster Tunnel. The monsters weren't real, but we were still a bit afraid.

The Animal Shed had animals you could pet. There were baby goats, sheep, rabbits, and a pony. We liked the itty-bitty pig the best.

Alf and Ettabetta got stuck at the top of the Ferris wheel. Alf couldn't look down. Ettabetta sat very still. Those two were glad when that ride was over.

We ate lunch under a big, shady oak tree. A band played terrific music by us.

Tic and Hot Rod clapped their hands and tapped their feet to the music.

Even the trash cans at Happy Land are fun.
When you step by Cubby, he speaks to you!
We fed Cubby some trash. *SWISH!* He ate it!

Feed your trash to me.

I'm crazy about this treat!

Cass got some fluffy cotton candy. It was sticky and sweet.

After lunch, we got Hot Rod's mom and dad to ride the Lucky Ducky. Those two looked silly sitting with the little kids. That made us giggle.

Tac and Oswald rode the Twist and Spin. It made them dizzy.

The Streak is the fastest ride at Happy Land. We waited and waited in line. But then we went lickety-split! We zipped up and down the tracks as fast as the wind. We screamed a lot! We had never been on a ride that fast.

Eeek!

The Streak
Admit One

Here we are on the way home.
We'll always remember this super day.

Unit 12

Memory Words   come   coming   they   our   put

Golly Is on the Ball

Golly was resting on the grass.
He stretched. He lay his face on the grass.
He began to fall asleep.

Then, *whiz!*
Golly could see the Superkids' basketball fly by.

Golly jumped over the wall.
He chased the ball and stopped it.

Golly tried to pick up the ball with his teeth.
But it was too big.

All the Superkids ran up.
Frits said, "Golly stopped the ball.
But his teeth made small holes in it."

"Oh, well," said Lily, "Golly can keep that ball.
We'll go to the mall and get a new one."

Play Ball!

The Superkids were having a good time at the shopping mall. First, they got a brand new basketball. Now they were going to see the Super Hawks. The basketball team was going to shoot some baskets outside the mall.

"I'm so glad the Super Hawks are coming here," said Lily.
"It will be fun to see them play."

"Come on," said Cass. "Let's all sit on this bench. We'll be close to the players."

"The Hawks are a super basketball team," said Hot Rod.

"I think that's why they're called the <u>Super</u> Hawks," said Lily, smiling.

"Here they come!" said Sal. "The team is starting to play!"

Number 2 passed the ball under the basket to Number 4. Number 4 jumped up and tossed the ball into the basket. *SWISH!* The Superkids clapped and yelled.

Then Number 6 got the ball. He dribbled quickly past Number 9 and shot a basket, too. The kids all grinned. "Way to go, Super Hawks!" they hollered.

Number 7 got the ball next. He ran and jumped way up with the ball in his hands.

"He's trying to do a slam dunk!" said Sal.

But the ball did not go in the basket. Number 7 slammed the ball on the rim and it popped out of his hands. Up, up, up it went.

The basketball sailed up over the top of a shop and the wall. It got stuck on top of the mall! Number 7 was hanging on to the rim, but then he fell.

When Number 7 fell,
Lily ran to him. "Are
you O.K.?" she asked.

"I'm fine," he said. "But
I lost our basketball."

"It's stuck up there,"
said Lily. "You can
play with our new
ball. The Superkids
just got it at the mall."

Number 7 looked
puzzled. "What's a
Superkid?" he asked.

The Superkids yelled,
"We're the Superkids!"

"Would the Superkids like to play with us?" asked Number 7.

"YES!" said Lily, jumping up and down.

Then she stopped. "But the Super Hawks are all so tall," she said. "We're too small to play basketball with you."

"You won't be too small now!" said Number 7. He picked up Lily.

"I'm super tall!" said Lily. "I can play with the Super Hawks!"

The other players picked up the rest of the Superkids.

"Play ball!" said Number 7.

"Play ball!" said Lily.

With the Super Hawks' help, the super tall Superkids shot lots of baskets. Lily even made a slam dunk!

The fans all clapped and yelled, "Go, Super Hawks! Go, Superkids!"

Up at Dawn

"I wish we could see animals like Tex McGraw does," said Tic.

"Yes," said Cass, "not just dull, tame animals like Golly."

Golly put his jaw on his paws. But Tic and Cass didn't see him acting sad.

Tic was saying to Cass, "Sleep over, and we'll get up at dawn and look for animals."

"O.K.!" said Cass.

The girls got up at dawn and went out to Tic's lawn.

"I feel awfully sleepy," said Cass with a big yawn.

Just then, they saw two little fawns.

"Aw!" whispered Tic. "They're cute."

The girls crawled closer.

Suddenly, Golly leaped up and the fawns ran off!

Cass giggled, "Golly showed us that he's not so dull and tame, didn't he?"

Tex McGraw's Visit

"Look at this," said Hot Rod. "Tex McGraw is coming."

"Tex McGraw!" said Cass. "I never miss his T.V. show!"

"I like it, too," said Tic. "He travels all over, and you see interesting animals."

"Why is he coming here?" asked Cass.

"He's picking the winner of the Grand Land Contest," said Hot Rod. "To win, your land has to look grand. No litter."

"What if Tex McGraw comes by our bus?" asked Tic.
"We have junk all over the lawn. It looks awful.
What will he think of us?"

"He'll think we are lazy Litter Critters," said Oswald.

"Let's tidy up the bus before Tex McGraw comes,"
said Hot Rod. "Perhaps we can win the Grand
Land Contest."

Tic, Tac, Toc, and Frits helped Oswald pick up trash. Alf and Doc scrubbed the bus. Ettabetta hung a planter, and Icky put plants in it. Sal and Hot Rod put up an awning with stripes. Lily and Cass got a bench. They put it under the awning.

"Our bus looks like new," said Oswald. "What will we get if we win the contest?"

"The winners get to be on T.V. with Tex McGraw," said Hot Rod.

Just then Lily saw a big van. "Look!" she yelled. "Tex McGraw is coming!"

The van stopped. A small man with a
big hat got out.

"Is that Tex McGraw?" asked Oswald.

"He has freckles, just like me," said Cass.

"He looks taller on T.V.," whispered Tic.

Tex asked the kids, "Did you all fix up this spot?"

Alf said, "Yes! We all did!"

"Well, my golly! It looks grand," said Tex.

Golly jumped up to kiss Tex.

"No, Golly," Cass said. "He wasn't calling you."

"All my fans would like to see this grand spot," said Tex. "You must be on T.V. with me. Yes, my golly, you win the Grand Land Contest."

The Superkids clapped and yelled. Golly wagged his tail.

Tex chuckled and called out, "Let's set up the show!"

When the show began, Tex said grand things about the work the Superkids did. Then he gave Alf a silver cup as a prize.

"The Superkids are the winners of the Grand Land Contest," Tex said. "You kids did a grand job cleaning up your spot. My golly, yes."

At that, Golly jumped up. He put his paws on Tex and kissed him on the chin.

"Well, my golly!" said Tex. "Isn't this grand? My golly!"

"Yup! Yup!" yapped Golly.

Unit 13

Memory Words   know   does   cold   laugh   both   again

Party Planning

How can my party be fun and different? We could go to the park and play sports! But that's not so different.

We could go see a marching band! I like loud horns and trumpets! But I don't know where a band is playing.

We could go to the kids' museum! It has a garden with a huge ant farm! But the museum is far away.

We may as well just stay home. But wait! We could pitch a tent in the yard! It can be our fort. We can look at the stars when it's dark. We can see the sun rise in the morning. Yes, that would be a fun party!

Slumber Party

Tic, Lily, and Cass set up a tent in Tic's backyard.

"We'll have a fantastic slumber party," said Tic.

"It's fun to sleep in a tent," said Cass.

"Yes!" said Tic.

But Lily didn't say a thing. This was the first time she had slept away from home, and she was sort of afraid.

The girls got in their sleeping bags and began to whisper. It was very dark.

"I know a story about a scary monster you'll both like," said Tic.

"Oh, no!" said Lily.

"Oh, yes!" said Cass.

Tic started telling the story.

One day a boy was going down the road when he saw a pot of silver. "My mom will be happy when she sees this!" he said. He put the pot under his arm and ran home.

But the boy didn't know that the silver belonged to a horrible monster! Later, when the boy went to sleep, the monster went looking for him.

"Whooo stole my pot of silver?" said the monster.

The boy woke up. "I must be dreaming!" he said. But the horrible monster came closer.

"Whooo stole my silver?" the monster asked again. The boy felt something cold tapping his leg. "Whooo stole my silver? Was it YOU?"

Just as Tic said, "Was it YOU?" in her story, she grabbed Lily.

"Eek!" screamed Lily.

"Yikes!" yelled Cass.

Then Tic and Cass began to laugh. But Lily did not.

"I liked that story," said Cass.

Lily didn't say a thing.

"Let's go to sleep," said Tic.

The girls snuggled in their sleeping bags so they wouldn't get cold. It was very still and very dark.

Lily couldn't sleep. She kept thinking about the scary story.

Then Lily felt something wiggle by the bottom of her sleeping bag.

There was something down there! It wiggled again.
Lily screamed and kicked the thing at the end of her
sleeping bag. Tic and Cass woke up.

"What is the matter?" said Tic. "Why are you
kicking my feet?"

"Oh," said Lily. "Are those your feet?" Then she
started to cry.

"I'm afraid of the dark," Lily said.

"Oh, I didn't know that," said Tic. "Let me help you."

Tic lifted the tent flaps. "Look up at the sky," she said.

Cass and Lily looked up and saw all the stars.

"When it's dark, remember that the stars are up there shining for you. Then you won't be afraid," said Tic.

"I like the way the stars sparkle," said Lily.

One big star seemed to wink at Lily. She smiled.

"Does that make you feel better?" asked Tic.

"Yes," said Lily. "I'm not so afraid."

In a little while, she was fast asleep.

Sal and the Fire Department

Sal likes to visit the fire department on Third Street. Stormy, the fire dog, always greets Sal first. *Arf! Arf!* Sal pets her soft fur.

The rest of the firefighters are happy to see Sal, too. He is teaching them how to speak Spanish. They each take a turn saying "Hola!" Some days Sal helps clean the fire trucks. They can get really dirty. Sal and the firefighters always laugh and tell jokes.

But when the alarm rings, the firefighters must go. Sal stands back so he won't get hurt. The trucks hurry off to the fire.

Fire!

Chapter 1

RING! RING!

Chief Flinn picked up the telephone. "Fire Department Number Six," he said. "What? I don't speak Spanish. Wait!"

"Does anybody know how to speak Spanish?" yelled the fire chief.

"I know Spanish," said Sal.

"Good," said the chief. "Come and speak to this girl."

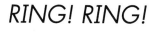

125

Sal spoke to the girl in Spanish. Then he said to the chief, "She says there is a fire on First Street!"

The fire chief rang the alarm.
The firefighters came running.
They put on their hats and coats
and jumped on the fire truck.

The truck rushed down
the street.

"Come with me," the fire chief said to Sal. "I'll need your help."

Sal jumped into the white car with the chief and they sped off.

Chapter 2

As the car turned onto First Street, Sal could see big puffs of gray smoke. Sal and the chief got out of the car. A girl ran up to both of them.

"My mom! My dad! My sisters and brothers!" yelled the girl in Spanish. "They are inside!"

"Quick!" yelled Sal to the chief. "Her family is trapped inside!"

"Hurry! Get the ladder up!" yelled the chief.

¡Mi mamá!
¡Mi papá!
¡Mis hermanos!
¡Están adentro!

The big ladder went up, up, up.

Some of the firefighters helped the family come down the ladder. Other firefighters sprayed the flames with hoses.

At last the fire was out. The family was a bit dirty, but no one was hurt. The mom and dad thanked the fire chief again and again.

Chapter 3

Just then, a reporter for the *Morning Star* came.

"Is the fire out?" asked the reporter.

"Yes!" said the chief. "And the family is safe."

"Good!" said the reporter. "It looks like you and your firefighters saved the day."

"We had a lot of help," said Chief Flinn. "If Sal and Carmen hadn't helped, the fire would have been a real disaster. They are both the real stars of the day."

"That is terrific," said the reporter. Then he asked Sal and Carmen to tell him what happened.

The next day, the story was in the *Morning Star*.

MORNING STAR NEWS

The day will be sunny and hot.

Two Kids Help Fire Department

A fire broke out Thursday in the home of the Vargas family on First Street. Carmen Vargas reported the fire. The rest of her family was trapped inside.

Luckily, Salvador Mirandez was visiting Fire Department 6 when Carmen called there. Carmen speaks only Spanish. Salvador explained to the chief what Carmen was saying.

Fire Chief Flinn said, "Without the help of both those children, that fire would have been a disaster!"

Unit 14

Memory Words   kind   buy   find   right   wash   light

The Garden Club

"Look!" said Alf. He pointed to the note. "Let's join the Garden Club!"

"Oh, boy!" said Toc. "I'll enjoy that!"

"First we'll get seeds," said Alf. "Then we'll plant them in the soil."

Toc said, "A sprinkler will keep the soil moist."

"And we'll pick weeds," said Alf. "Weeds annoy me! They spoil a garden."

"We have lots to do!" said Toc. "Let's ask the Superkids to help us!"

For the Birds

Chapter 1

"Who wants to plant a garden?" asked Toc.

"I do!" said all the Superkids.

"Terrific!" said Alf. "We just have to buy seeds."

Hot Rod said, "But I don't have a single coin."

"We can use coins from the club bank," said Doc.

"Toc and I will get a garden plot," said Alf.
"The rest of you can buy the seeds."

Alf and Toc ran to the Garden Club.
Lots of boys and girls were waiting
to get garden plots.

"Let's join the line," said Alf.

Alf and Toc had to wait a long,
long time.

At last it was Alf and Toc's turn. The gardener gave them plot number four. She said, "Your plot is right here." And she pointed to it on the map.

"Thank you!" said Alf and Toc. They rushed back to the bus.

Chapter 2

"We got a plot!" said Alf.
"Did you get seeds?"

Hot Rod said, "Yes! Tac and
I got corn seeds. Oswald and
Lily got carrot seeds. Ettabetta
and Sal are planting beans."

"Peas for Tic and me," said Doc.

"Radishes for me!" yelled Frits.

"And beets for Icky and me!"
said Cass.

"What kind of seeds did you get for Alf and me?" asked Toc.

"Oh, no!" said Doc.
"We forgot you!"

Alf and Toc were disappointed. They had waited in line so long! "Well," said Toc. "You can start planting without us. Alf and I will go find some seeds."

"I wish we could buy seeds," said Toc. "But there are no coins left."

"My mom puts birdseed in our bird feeder," said Alf. "We could plant some of that."

"Let's try it," said Toc.

Alf lifted Toc up. She grabbed a handful of birdseed.

Alf and Toc went to the garden.

Toc pointed to a spot. "Let's plant our seeds there," she said. "They will get lots of light."

Chapter 3

"What are you planting?" asked Sal.

"Birdseed!" said Toc.

The kids laughed.

"Are you going to grow birds?" giggled Tic.

"Tweet, tweet!" laughed Tac.

Toc and Alf planted their birdseed.
They kept the soil moist.
Each day they checked to see
if the birdseed had started to grow.

"How is your tweet weed?" laughed Cass.

"Do you have bird blossoms yet?" giggled Icky.

"Those kids annoy me," said Toc.

"Me too!" said Alf. "I don't enjoy their jokes."

After a while, carrots, radishes, corn, beans, peas, and beets started to grow. Something even began to grow from the birdseed!

Each day the birdseed plants got bigger.
In fact, they were the tallest plants in
the garden! The kids stopped making fun
of Alf and Toc. Then, one sunny day,
the birdseed plants blossomed!

"That birdseed plant is so pretty!" said Doc.

"It's the best plant in the garden," said Tac.

Just then a bird landed on the plant. Toc laughed. She said, "See? We DID grow birds after all!"

The Winner's Mitt

Ettabetta's softball team was about to play the Giants. She said, "The Giants are the best team in the city."

Ettabetta looked at her mitt. "I have had this mitt for ages!" she said. "It is a mess. Mice ate the laces. There is a huge rip in the center. I left it out in the rain twice, so it has spots in places."

Ettabetta looked at the mitt in The Sports Shop.
"The Winner's Mitt is nice and fancy," she said.
"But the price is too much. I have only three dollars
and some change. Let's face it: I'm stuck with
my mitt. Let's hope it's a winner's mitt, too!"

The Lost Mitt

Chapter 1

"That's a nice baseball mitt, Frits," Ettabetta said.

"Yes, it's pretty good," said Frits as he punched it.

"I have been saving money to buy a new mitt," said Ettabetta. "I could really use one today. My team is playing the best team in the city."

"I'll lend you my mitt," said Frits.

"You will?" said Ettabetta. "Thanks, Frits."

The game was exciting. Ettabetta's team was winning by one point. Ettabetta punched Frits's mitt and whispered, "Come on, mitt, we can do it. One more catch and we win the game."

WHAM! The batter hit the ball way up into the sky.

"Catch it!" yelled Ettabetta's team.

Ettabetta whipped off her face mask. She raced to the left, then back. Then she stretched and held the mitt up.

THUD!

The ball landed right in the center of the mitt. Ettabetta's team clapped and cheered. Ettabetta had a huge grin.

Chapter 2

That evening, Ettabetta could hardly sleep. She kept remembering her fantastic catch. "I would never have won the game without Frits's magic mitt," she said to herself.

Suddenly, she sat up. "Frits's mitt!" she said. "Oh, no! I left it at the ballpark. I must look for it in the morning."

Just as it got light, Ettabetta went to the ballpark. She looked everywhere for the mitt. But she couldn't find it anyplace.

"This is awful," said Ettabetta. "Frits will be so mad. What can I do?"

Then she remembered her savings. "Maybe I can earn some extra money. Then I can buy Frits the same kind of mitt. Maybe he won't even know that it is not his mitt."

THE BIG
G
Gus and Gert's Garage
Tires Checked
Repairs

Chapter 3

Ettabetta did some work for Gus and Gert. First she had to wash a bunch of cars. Then she put out the trash. By the end of the morning, she had earned the money she needed.

Ettabetta raced to the sports shop. She paid for the new mitt.

Ettabetta saw Frits at the bus.
She tossed the new mitt to him and
said, "Frits, your mitt was super.
Thanks a lot."

Frits looked surprised. He said,
"This is a nice mitt, Ettabetta.
But it's not mine."

Ettabetta gulped. "It is now,"
she said sadly. "I lost yours, so
I had to buy this one to replace it."

"But, Ettabetta," Frits said, "I have my mitt. Icky picked it up right after the game. He gave it to me this morning."

"Really?" said Ettabetta.

"Really," said Frits. He tossed the new mitt to Ettabetta and smiled. "But now you have the mitt you wanted. Let's play catch!"

Unit 15

ou		ow = Ow!		Story Words
loud	sounds	wow	clowns	parade
round	pounded	town	crowns	tuba
ground	shouted	brown	flowers	clarinets
		crowd	cowgirl	

ou		ow = Ow!		Story Words
found	shouted	how	frown	house
sounds	loudly	now	crowded	Ms.
around	grouchy	down	Powers	surprise
		wow		

ow = ō					Story Word
snow	snowy	own	blowing	snowballs	leaves
show	throw	low	bowling	slow	

ou		ow = Ow!	ow = ō	Story Words
sound	out	how	slow	magazine
counted	our	now	shows	goes
shouted		wow	window	water
loudly		frowning		
ground		scowled		

Memory Words warm walk give once done

The Parade Marches By

The town was having a big parade.

"Here come the clowns!" Oswald shouted.

The clowns did silly tricks. The crowd laughed and clapped. A cowgirl rode by on a brown pony. Little kids tossed flowers on the ground. Next came a king and queen with sparkling crowns.

Then the kids heard the stomp, stomp of a marching band. Drummers pounded on big, round drums. Loud trumpets blasted. The tubas made big, huge sounds. Flutes and clarinets played fast, fun tunes.

"Wow!" said Cass. "The marching band is the best part!"

The Lesson

"Hot Rod has been to the bus only once this week," said Cass. "What could he be doing?"

Oswald said, "I saw him just now. He wouldn't tell me where he was going. He was grouchy about it, too."

"Maybe he needs help," said Cass. "Let's find him."

Cass and Oswald found Hot Rod's bike by a house down the street. Cass said, "Let's see what Hot Rod is doing in there."

Cass and Oswald peeked in the house.
They heard a tune coming from inside.

> Bee bop ditty ditty wow wow,
> Bee bop ditty ditty wonk wonk!

A woman said, "You made a mistake,
Hot Rod. Try it once again."

> Bee bop ditty ditty wow wow,
> Bee bop ditty ditty wonk wonk!

"Oh, no," said Hot Rod. "The clarinet is
too hard, Ms. Powers. I want to quit."

Ms. Powers said, "Don't give up. You have done so well. I want you to play in the talent show on Saturday."

"But I just want to quit," said Hot Rod with a frown.

"Give it a try," said Ms. Powers. "If you still want to quit after the show, I will understand."

"Well, O.K.," said Hot Rod. "But I hope my pals don't come. I don't want them to make fun of me."

"Let's go," whispered Cass.

Later, Cass said, "It's terrific that Hot Rod plays the clarinet. Let's go to the show with all the kids."

"O.K.," said Oswald. "But let's not tell them about Hot Rod. It will be a surprise."

Chapter 2

Saturday came. The Superkids walked to the show.

First a girl played the drums very loudly.

BANG! BANG! BLAM! BLAM!

Then a boy sang a song.

Sal yawned.

Ettabetta wiggled. "Why did you make us come?" she asked Cass.

"You'll see," said Cass.

Then two girls played trumpets.

Wop wop blat blat blat!

It was getting warm. Alf began to squirm in his seat. "This is boring," he whispered to Sal. "When will it be done?"

Just then, a boy began to play a jazzy tune.

Bee bop ditty ditty wow wow,
Bee bop ditty ditty wow wow wow!

"It is Hot Rod!" said Icky. "I didn't know he could play the clarinet!"

"Wow! He sounds really good!" said Doc.

175

The crowd enjoyed the song.
When Hot Rod was done, they
all clapped loudly.

After the show, Ms. Powers said,
"Thank you, Hot Rod. You played
very well. How do you feel about
the clarinet now?"

"It's not so bad," said Hot Rod.
"But I still want to give up
my lessons."

Just then, the Superkids crowded around Hot Rod.
They all shouted at once.

Hot Rod, you're terrific!

Is it hard?

We didn't know you could play the clarinet!

Show us how.

"Can you give me clarinet lessons, Hot Rod?" asked Cass.

"Yes," said Hot Rod. "But first I have to take more lessons myself! It feels good to play well, even if it takes time and hard work." He gave Ms. Powers a warm smile. Then he began to play.

Summer Snow

The Superkids planned to meet at the park to play tag.
Tic and Tac were the first to show up.

"Let's play catch with my ball while we wait," said Tic.

"I have my own ball," said Tac.

"O.K.," said Tic. "Let's throw both balls back and forth.
We can pretend they're snowballs!"

"Snow? On a summer day like this?" asked Tac.
"It's hot, and there isn't even any wind blowing!"

"Just pretend it's snowy," said Tic.

So Tac tossed her ball low and slow. It looked like
she was bowling! But Tic tossed her ball up and it
hit a branch so hard that a bunch of leaves fell on
the girls.

Tac laughed. "Look!" she said. "It's snowing!"

That Was Yesterday

One warm day, the Superkids were playing tag.

"I'm It!" shouted Frits. He counted, "1, 2, 3, 4, 5, 6, 7, 8, 9, 10! Look out! Here I come!"

Alf raced past Frits. "You can't catch me! You can't catch me!" teased Alf.

Frits chased Alf. When he got close, Frits reached out his hand. "I got you, Alf! Now you're It!" shouted Frits.

"I am not!" said Alf loudly. "You missed me by a mile."

"I did not! I tagged you!" yelled Frits.

"You never came close," shouted Alf.
"I'm not as slow as you are!"

Alf and Frits began to push each other.
They fell to the ground.

"Stop it!" said Lily.

"You'll get hurt!" said Hot Rod.

But Alf and Frits did not stop. The kids
had to split apart the two boys.

Ettabetta said, "Come on, you two. Be nice. Let's play tag."

"No! I quit!" said Frits. "I'm not playing tag with a cheater."

"I quit, too!" yelled Alf. "I'm going home."

The rest of the kids just sat there frowning.

Sal said, "This is no fun. They have spoiled the game for us, too."

"Let's just go," said Toc. The kids split up and walked home.

The next day the kids met at the bus. Frits and Alf scowled and scowled at each other.

"It is too warm to play tag," Toc said. "Let's go fishing!"

Alf said, "I'm not going if Frits goes."

"And I'm not going if Alf goes," said Frits.

Toc got angry. "You spoiled our game yesterday,"
she said. "But you are not going to spoil our fishing
trip. You can both just stay here!"

The kids left for the pond. Frits and Alf were left
on the bus.

"Now look what you have done," said Alf.

"You started it," said Frits.

"I did not," said Alf.

"You did, too," said Frits.

"Oh, I wish you would just go home," grumbled Alf.

"I got here first!" shouted Frits.

"O.K., then stay. But I'm not speaking to you," said Alf. He picked up a magazine and began to read it.

Frits just looked out the window.

Chapter 3

For a long time Frits and Alf did not make a sound.

Then Alf said softly, "Wow!"

Frits asked, "What?"

"Look at this!" said Alf. "This magazine shows how to make a rocket that can really fly!"

"Let me see!" said Frits. Alf handed him the magazine. "Wow, that's terrific," said Frits.

"All you need is a plastic bottle, cardboard, tape, a cork, water, and a bike pump," said Alf.

Frits said, "I have all those things at home. Let's walk there and get them!"

"O.K.!" said Alf.

As Frits and Alf left the bus, they bumped into Sal.

"Where are you two going?" Sal asked.

"We're going to get things we need for a super project," said Frits.

Sal said, "But aren't you still mad at each other? I didn't think you two were speaking."

Alf and Frits looked at each other. At once they began to laugh.

"Well…that was yesterday," said Alf.

Unit 16

Memory Words   live   eight   old   hold   write

The Superkids Like Books!

Cass likes cookbooks. She is reading a book called *Good Food for Kids.*

Sal likes to read about sports. He's reading *How to Play Better Football.*

Oswald likes animals. He's reading about how to be a zookeeper.

Ettabetta likes joke books. She is reading *Goofy Jokes and Foolish Riddles.*

Lily likes spooky books that make her shiver.
She just finished *An Owl Hoots at the Moon.*

Hot Rod likes *Zoom!* It's about fast cars.

Alf likes camping. His book is called
Hiking in the Woods.

Tac is reading *Little Red Riding Hood.*
She likes books about brave girls.

The Case of the
Mystery Monster

Lily took some books to the checkout desk at the library.

"You must like mystery books," Mr. Burns said.

"Oh, yes," Lily said. "I do!"

"You aren't the only one!" said Mr. Burns. "Eight new mystery books are missing from the library."

"Who took them?" asked Lily.

"I have only one clue," Mr. Burns said. "I found this note."

The note said,

Hold on to your books!
The Mystery Monster lives here!

"Monster?" said Lily. "How could a monster live here?"

"I don't know," said Mr. Burns.

"Perhaps I can help," Lily said. "I'll come every day and look for the Mystery Monster."

"Thank you, Lily," said Mr. Burns.

The next day, Lily went back to the library. "Hi, Mr. Burns," she said. "Are there any notes from the Mystery Monster?"

"No," said Mr. Burns. "But another book is missing!"

"I'll sit next to the mystery shelf," said Lily.
"Perhaps I'll spot the monster."

Lily sat down and opened her book. She was
reading *The Mystery of the Eight Old Lost Bones.*

Lily peeked over her book at everyone in the library. No one looked like a Mystery Monster.

Then around noon, Lily saw a man in a brown coat walk over to the mystery bookshelf. The man just stood there for a second. Then he walked on to the sports books.

"That man does not seem interested in mystery books," Lily said to herself.

Lily got up and took a walk around the room. She still didn't spot any clues.

So she went back to her table to get her book. But her book had vanished! There was a note in its place.

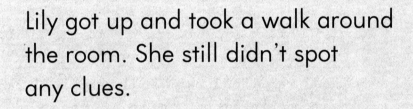

Hold on to your books! The Mystery Monster lives here!

Lily whirled around. The man in the brown coat was walking quickly out of the room.

Lily ran over to Mr. Burns. "Mr. Burns!" she whispered. "Stop that man! He's the Mystery Monster!"

Mr. Burns jumped up from his desk. Books tumbled to the ground.

The man in the brown coat went outside.

"Oh, no," said Lily. "Now we'll never catch the Mystery Monster!"

Mr. Burns looked very upset. "Oh no," he said. "Perhaps I let my foolish joke go too far. Let me show you, Lily."

He took out a big sheet of paper from under his desk. It said:

Boys and Girls!
Coming Soon!
Mystery Book Week!
We'll have a Mystery Book Club and a Mystery Book Corner.
All mystery book fans invited!
The Mystery Monster

"You see, Lily," said Mr. Burns. "Mystery Book Week is coming in eight days. I took all the mystery books for the Mystery Corner. I wrote the spooky notes myself."

"Oh, so you are the Mystery Monster," said Lily with a giggle.

"Yes," said Mr. Burns. "But now all the other kids will know the secret."

"No, they won't," said Lily with a smile. "I won't tell. After all, I enjoy a good mystery!"

Ettabetta's E-mail

Ettabetta sent this e-mail:

Dear Superkids,

If you come to the zoo
Today at two,
You'll see what I've done
To give you some fun.

I have riddles to tease you
And prizes to please you.

I promise I've planned
A game that is grand.

It's not a bore.
It's not a chore.
(I can't say more.)

So leave your work
And leave your worry,
And come to the zoo at two.
Hurry, scurry!

Love,

Ettabetta

Send

Zoo Clue

"Where is Ettabetta?" asked Toc. "She asked us to meet her here at the zoo."

"Maybe she's inside," said Cass. "Let's go find her."

The kids went to the ticket booth.

"Are you the Superkids?" asked the lady in the booth.

"Yes," said Icky.

"I have something to give you," said the lady. She handed Icky a note.

Icky read the note to the kids.

Dear Superkids,

This is an animal riddle game. Read each riddle, and figure out which animal it is about. Go to that animal and there will be another riddle for you. Solve all the riddles, and I'll give you a nice prize.

Love,
Ettabetta

"Look!" said Hot Rod. "The first riddle is on the back."

I live in the desert.
I have a huge hump.
You can ride on my back.
I'm kind of a grump.

"It sounds like a camel!"
said Frits.

"Yes! Let's find one,"
said Cass.

The Superkids went past the
giraffes and the gorilla. They
looked at the seals swimming
in a pool. A zookeeper let Doc
feed a fish to a seal.

Gorilla

At last the kids found the camels.

"These camels aren't really grumps," laughed Frits. "They are just hungry!"

"Look, here is another note," said Hot Rod.

"Cows give milk," said Oswald.

"And cows moo!" said Lily. "Let's find a cow."

I give milk,
And I say "moo."
I live on a farm,
But I'm here at the zoo.

? ?

The kids found a gentle
cow and another note.

"Read it, Oswald!" said Cass.

I have two big ears
And a coat of brown.
I fly when it is dark,
And I hang upside down.
? ? ?

"A coat of brown means its fur is brown," said Oswald.

"If it has two big ears and brown fur, it could be a rabbit," said Sal.

"But rabbits don't fly," said Tac. "It must be a bird."

"But birds don't have big ears," said Toc.

"Owls look like they have ears. And they fly!" said Tac.

"But owls never hang upside down," said Icky. "Hold it! I know! It's a bat."

The kids raced to the bat house. Inside, seven or eight bats were flying around.

"I don't like this place," said Cass, "Let's please get out of here!"

"Wait!" said Oswald.
"Ettabetta left another note."

> This note is not a clue.
> If you go to the Petting Zoo,
> There will be a prize for you.
> Ettabetta will be there, too.

"I love prizes!" said Hot Rod.
"Let's go!"

The Superkids ran to the
Petting Zoo.

"What took you so long?" said Ettabetta.

"Some of your riddles were tricky," said Tic.

I live in the desert.
I have a huge hump.
You can ride on my back.
I'm kind of a grump!

I give milk.
And I say "moo."
I live on a farm,
But I'm here at the zoo!

I have two big ears
And a coat of brown.
I fly when it is dark
And I hang upside down.

"What is our prize?" asked Hot Rod. "Is it food?"

"Just look at the red letters in all the riddles," said Ettabetta. "Put them together to make two words that tell what the prize is."

The kids tried to make two words with the red letters.

"I have it!" said Sal.
"It's ZOO BALLOONS!"

217